God, Did You Send This Mate to Me?

CYNTHIA MARIE BOLTON

Order this book online at www.trafford.com
or email orders@trafford.com

Most Trafford titles are also available at major online book retailers.

Printed in the United States of America.

ISBN: 978-1-4269-9734-1 (sc)
ISBN: 978-1-4269-9735-8 (e)

Library of Congress Control Number: 2011917587

Trafford rev. 09/29/2011

www.trafford.com

North America & international
toll-free: 1 888 232 4444 (USA & Canada)
phone: 250 383 6864 • fax: 812 355 4082

Contents

Introduction

Over the years I've had the opportunity to observe many different marriages from a close proximity. In doing so, I've learned that though they all differ in many ways, there are also many similarities. The areas of concerns that I've seen in these different relationships are basically stem from the same kinds of problems.

Amos 3 and 3 of the King James Version of the Holy Bible reads can two walk together, except they be agreed? So if two cannot even walk together unless they agree, how can they live together?

I hope that when you have finished reading this book, you will be inspired to look deeper into what you are about to enter into, or perhaps what you've already entered. If you are not yet married, you will begin to seek understanding first of yourself and what you expect out of marriage, what you have to offer to the marriage, and finally are you willing to take on a life long compromise with another individual. Secondly, you will begin to seek understanding of the mate that you will vow to spend the rest of your mortal life with. Does he/she share any of the same values and ideas about life as you do? Can you find common ground when there is a disagreement between the two of you? If you are already married, and you have opened the door of reality, you've seen that to have a successful marriage, it's going to take a lot of work. Are you willing to work on making your marriage great, or have you already considered ending it? Does your marriage consist of just the two of you, or have you invited Christ to head up your union?

Over the years, people have lost the true value of marriage. Marriage was designed by God to be sacred and forever. It should not be entered into lightly nor dismissed so easily. The divorce rate is so high, because mankind has failed to take the sanctity of marriage serious. There is only one acceptable reason for entering marriage, and only that one thing that will seal the marriage and that is LOVE. God is love, and those that He joined together, let no man put asunder. So seek your answer from the one that knows all, God. Ask him the question, "*God, Did You Send This Mate to Me?*"

Chapter One

Who Shows Us How to be Married?

Observing your parents, as you grow up, influences your perception of marriage in a tremendous way. It has a bearing on what most of you expect out of your spouse and on what kind of spouse you will become. Most people have only their parents, grandparents, or some couple within their family that they use as role models for their own marriage. However unconscious the imitating may be, most people find themselves duplicating the roles of some married relative. Unfortunately, not all couples had the golden opportunity to get the proper counseling that they needed prior to entering into a marriage. Prenuptial counseling would be beneficial to a marriage. It would help the couple to really tap into hidden matters of the heart, of not only the other person but of one's self.

Yes, we are taught by our parents and others, how marriage is supposed to be.

If daddy curses at mommy and hits her, a lot of children grow up to consider that a normal part of marriage. If that son, watches daddy treat his mother any kind of way, more than likely, he will treat his spouse the same. The same with the daughters, they do not expect very much from their husbands, because they have seen the things that mommy took from daddy. In this story that I am about to share, you will see exactly what I'm talking about.

Once upon a time, there was a little girl and her brother who lived with their parents. We will call the little girl Sally. Sally's brother, Joe was younger than she. Every time that mommy would leave daddy and go stay with grandma, Sally would take her doll, Sissy with her and tell Sissy that it's going to be okay. Joe would always ask mommy if he could stay behind with daddy. Mommy would reply, "No Joe, your daddy is drunk and acting real stupid, let's go." With this kind of thing happening at least two to three times a month, the children began to think nothing of it. However, unknowingly, it was having a profound affect on Sally. Sally would grip her doll very tightly during her parent's argument as if the doll was afraid. The doll was actually symbolic to her. She was afraid, and wanted someone to hold her and tell her that it would be all right. Well, as Sally and Joe continue to grow up in this home, they too began to develop violent behavior when dealing with conflict. They would fight among themselves as a solution to their problems.

Sally turned 16 and she thought she was ready to start dating. Well needless to say, her parents never got any better at communicating so her example remained the same her whole childhood. Sally comes home one day with her blouse ripped on the shoulder. When asked by her brother, Joe what had happened, she stated that, "oh it was nothing, my boyfriend just got angry with me and tore my top". Sally never reported this incidence to any adult, and neither did Joe. Neither of the teenagers, found the incidence to be anything out of the ordinary. As time went on, Sally dated boy after boy that would rough her up and some even beat on her. All Joe had to say about it was that Sally ought to act right, because he would handle up on his girlfriend, if she did not do as he wanted her to. One Sunday evening, Sally invited her boyfriend, John to dinner with her parents. At this time she decided to tell her parents that she and John were engaged to be married. Daddy asked John where do you work? Do you have your own house, and things of that sort? Never once did they advice their daughter to get any prenuptial counseling. So as you could imagine, Sally had no idea what she was about to get herself involved with.

The honeymoon consisted of several weekends of loud parties with John's drinking buddies. Sally tried to please John by keeping thing tidy up after him and his friends. She tolerated this behavior for about a year and a half. One day, Sally decided to confront John about his actions. She tried to explain to him how she was feeling neglected and used by him and his friends. John jumped up slapped her in the mouth, and told her that she was not to talk to him that way. Only weeks later, Sally learned that she was pregnant, but was afraid to tell John because she didn't know how he would react.

Meanwhile, Joe, Sally's brother, comes to Sally's door with his bag in his hand, saying "Sis, I need a place to bunk, my old lady done kick me out". Sally invited Joe in and asked him what had happened. He told her that he and his girlfriend had a fight and the girlfriend made him hit her. Sally replied, "oh she'll cool down in a few days and take you back, that's how I do John". She invited Joe to stay a few days with her and John, without first consulting John. Needless to say, when John got home, he was not pleased. He told Joe he had to go. Sally again tried to reason with John which caused a big fight between the two of them resulting in a miscarriage for Sally. John of course blamed Sally for not informing him that she was carrying "his child".

Five years have passed, and Sally and John have had two children. Joe has finally settled down and married a young woman. Both the siblings' marriage was in trouble. To make a long story short, after only six and a half years of marriage, Sally and John get a divorce. Sally now has sole custody of the two children, without very much support for John. Joe is currently serving a life sentence for accidentally killing his spouse during a domestic dispute between the two. Sally's children being young, gives her a chance to remarry and show her children what God has intended for marriage to truly be, or can she, when she simply doesn't know how?

This story is only one scenario of what comes out of families that have unhealthy and broken marriages. Do you want your child/children to follow such examples for their marriages? Are you setting a true example to your children? Are there other ways Sally can learn how a marriage is supposed to be? Yes, I'm sure there are other authors that have had the ideal to write a book to share guidance and wisdom about how to know if you are with the right mate, and how to make it work, once you have entered into the sanctity of marriage. Even after growing up in such homes as Sally and Joe, there is hope for children like those to grow up and to have very healthy and successful marriages. How can couples like these two beat the odds and have a successful marriage. First, they must acknowledge that their parents had an unhealthy marriage. They must decide that they will expect and have more out of their own marriage. It has been said, that a person is drawn to mates that share similar characteristics of his mother if the person is a male and of her father if the person is a female. So if one sees that he or she is repetitiously dating a person that act like his or her father or mother, that person needs to seek guidance counseling on why he or she is attractive to such individuals. I am a strong believer that a person can achieve whatever he or she believes that he or she can achieve. However, the person to convince is one's own self. So in other words, an individual must heal and find closure from scars created in his or her mind and spirits by broken marriages that they were unfortunate enough to witness and be a part of.

Chapter Two

The True Reason To Get Married

There is a play and movie already out there, entitled *Why Did I Get Married.* Well the points that I would like to address in this chapter will be focusing on the reasons people get married as opposed to wondering why after getting married the marriage seems to not be working. People get married for various reasons. Some want to escape from their home life. Some want financial security. Some don't want to co-habitat, which to them is living in sin. Some are concerned about not fitting in with what society thinks. Finally some get married because they're in love.

God ordained marriage as a sacred commitment between two people who love one another. Yet, some people enter into that union lightly and for the wrong reasons. Yes I know that many people have gotten married because they created a child together out of wedlock. Some of those marriages survived, but not the majority of them. It is only right that a child or children grow up in a home with two loving parents. However, loving parents are those that are kind and civil to each other. Not those who curse and fuss continually around their children making life miserable. It is important that one considers how marrying a person that he or she doesn't love will affect the children that are involved. Two people must find out how compatible they are to one another or in other words are they good for one another. This is important to avoiding the vicious cycle that will begin when they rear a family with a broken marriage. Again, the children learn from their parents how to be married, how to treat their spouses. So, if it is not smart to marry a person because you share a child with him or her, what do you do about giving your child a home with a mom and a dad? Again, a child is better off in a happy home. In an ideal world, all children will have two parents, but two parents that constantly fuss and fight are not healthy for children. Let's remember that biological parents are not the only parents that can give children the loving home they deserve. There are many adoptive parents and stepparents that provide safe warm environments for their children.

Another reason people have gotten married is for financial security. Yes, we all want to feel safe and be taken care of by someone. There are still some people who want to be independent only to depend on themselves for their livelihoods. However, there are many more that want someone to be the sole provider especially women who dream and fantasize about the husband who will one day make all their dreams come true. Money is good and we all need it, however, it is not the glue that will hold a marriage together. As a matter of fact, finances are one of the leading causes to the rise in the divorce rates. A woman meets a man who seems to be doing very well financially and promises her the world; she considers nothing else or no one else. All she can think about is the fact that he has plenty of money, and that he has chosen her to share his life as well as his money. However, do they love one another? Once two individuals have join as husband and wife, sometimes because of financial security, neither person in the marriage will admit that the marriage is not working, and that there is not enough common ground to make it work. So these two individuals will hang on to the marriage and make not only each other miserable, but also cause irreversible damage to their children. There is an old cliché that says "It's cheaper to keeper her". So some men will not get a divorce because they are afraid they will be ordered not only pay child support, but also spousal support. Again money is not the glue to a successful marriage, but it has kept many couples hanging on to a mockery of a marriage.

Religion plays a very enormous part in many people reasoning for getting married. They want so bad to be with someone and to please the church and others in their religious arena. So, they hurry up and tie the knot. This knot is bound to break yet they do it anyway. They are pressured because they are living in sin and they need to do the right thing. I agree, we shouldn't live in sin, however, it is not a valid reason for taking such a big step and entering into a union that is suppose to be sacred. Before we take such a serious step, we must consider that this is supposed to be a lifetime commitment. There are many religious beliefs about how couples are supposed to conduct themselves. There are even religious beliefs about ending a marriage. Misguided religion can have devastating affects on the lives of many. It is important that every individual has his or her own relationship with his or her higher power. Getting married to legalize sex is not enough to keep a marriage strong and successful. What about when the honeymoon stage is over, what is left after the physical attraction has simmered down?

So in other words, pressuring another person to marry you because you don't want to live in sin is a colossal mistake. No, I'm not saying to continue living in sin, but I am saying, stop the sinning and start praying for God to give you and your potential mate guidance on what to do next. Tell your mate that you don't want to live in sin, but that you will only get married if that's what both of you feel is right to do and you feel that you have gotten approval from God who knows all.

Well what is the true reason to get married? LOVE is the only reason that two people should enter into such a sacred union. Even with love, couples have to work at keeping their marriage alive and healthy. It is really a struggle when there is no love presence. Marriage is a commitment that involves two people in one another lives for the rest of their lives. Day after day, year after year, until death do them apart. One has to love another in order to tolerate the unfavorable behaviors that are possessed by all individuals. Regardless of how much a person may love his or her mate, there will be some flaws in that individual. It takes love to look beyond one another's faults. It is only love that will help two people to weather a stormy time within the marriage. It is so easy to pass blame and to throw accusations as to whose fault it is. However, love will allow the two to sit down and empathize with each other. It will cause each to put aside what he or she feels and to try and understand what the other person is feeling. During the courting stage and the engagement stage, most people try to walk a chalk line for their mate. Men are on their best behavior, and women work extra hard to keep that beautiful look that first attracted that man. However, once the dust has settled from the honeymoon, those individual begin to see more and more flaws in their mates. Here is a short story that will reiterate what I've already said in this chapter.

Once upon a time there were these two neighbors that sat on the front porch of one of their houses and took a stroll down memory lane. These two individuals had been wives for over twenty-five years. They shared with each other the ups and downs of marriage. Wife number one is Isabel and wife number two is Ester. Well Isabel began to tell Ester of how she met and married her husband, Josh. She said that she lived with parents that were very strict on her and hardly allowed her to socialize with the opposite sex. So needless to say she was dying to get out of their clutches. Well low and behold, she met Josh one day at the supermarket. He was a salesman dressed in a nice business suit. She bumped into his brief case with her buggy and that's how it began. He asked for her number and before long they were engaged. She said all he had to offer her was freedom from that prison that she lived in. Only one year after meeting they were married. She said that she was only 18 years old when she tied the knot. She began to tell how challenging it was to live with this man and all of his strange expectations of her. She found it hard to accept that he believed that she was to do only what he thought was best. There was no discussion about what was best for the marriage. He had all the answers. When she would voice an opinion things would get real sticky in their marriage. He was not open-minded to any of her feelings or suggestions. They had two children together, and he had one outside the marriage that he got during an affair while they were married. Well, Isabel had to help him rear this child also. He told her if she loved him, she had to love his child. As time went on she began to realize that she had trade one prison for another.

Well, Ester began to share her experience as a wife, which was quiet different. She told how she and her husband Kyle met at a party hosted by some of her friends. She said that she was not looking to meet anyone at that time, but she did, not knowing that he would be her soul mate. She said as time went on they became very close friends. She said she enjoyed getting to know him and learning exactly how much they had in common. She said that he respected her feelings and belief on every issue that they would face. She said that they didn't always agree on things initially but that they were always able to reach some sort of agreement or compromise. She said they both work hard at keeping the lines of communication open because they wanted a peaceable marriage. She said one of their greater challenges was when they had their three children. Because of their differences in how they were reared by their parents, they didn't see eye to eye on how to rear their children. However challenging it was, it only drew them closer to one another because they loved each other enough to respect each others feelings and concerns about their disciplinary measures; including the rules and guidelines that they set for their children. They both agreed that when an issue would occur, that they would discuss it with one another before bring it to the children. This was to keep down misunderstandings and fights. Ester went on to smile as she said the name Kyle. She said that she had no regrets of their last twenty-five years as a couple. She did admit that there are some things that she looks back on that she would have done differently. Hind-sight is always 20/20 however, she still feel that her marriage has been very successful. Both the women were still in their marriage. Isabel was just trying to make the best of her situation, while Ester was yet enjoying her life with her family. It was not that both marriages didn't have their unique challenges, but both marriages were not united by love. Only one of the marriages was sealed by love. It is a fact, that love is the entire life—line to a successful marriage. I did not say that a marriage couldn't survive without love, but it will not be a true representation of what God has ordained as a sacred union. Many marriages yet exist without love. Not only are the spouses suffering, but those that are touched by the lives of those spouses, such as children and extended family members are affected also. What can I say? If it's not for love, it's not for real.

Chapter Three

Be Not Unequally Yoked

To all bible readers, we know the scripture tells us to be not unequally yoked.

When choosing a mate, one must consider how compatible the mate is for him or her. Do the both share enough of the same values in life? Can the both find common ground in times of controversy? Physical attraction is good, but it is not enough to build a relationship upon. When two people meet and they are physically attracted to one another it can lead to a relationship. Because the two are so excited that the chemistry is there, they think that they have found the real thing, but how much do they know about each other. What are their thoughts on bigger issues in life such as religion, abortions, capital punishment, child-rearing, divorce, and other life altering conditions?

Prior to marriage, it is not unusual for a mate to avoid disclosing his or her true feelings about a situation. This is because he or she doesn't want to cause any disturbance or controversy. He or she likes the good time that the two of them are having. Then after the two have decided to get married, so many issues that they can't see eye-to-eye develop. The marriage began to encounter very difficult times. The couple, not realizing that they need counseling, goes on with the unresolved issues and matters become even worse. Soon they have children and things are even more complicated. Now those values that they feel so differently about must be taught to their children. Whose values will the children learn, Dad's or Mom's? One can truly see where this could be the beginning of the end. Why? Simply because when it was just the two of them, they could just avoid discussing the situation with one another and each keep believing what he or she believes and let the other person believe whatever. Now that there are children and they want to know what to do in life about certain things, how do they seek the guidance from their parents, when that guidance is distorted by the parent's different values?

Of course every couple will have some differences. However, are the differences too great for the two as a couple to overcome? Can one mate respect the opinion of the other mate? Is one mate so opinionated that he or she will not even consider the thoughts and feelings of the other mate? When a couple comes to that point in the relationship where they cannot understand what the other is feeling or even why he or she is feeling that way, that's when the two should pray together and seek guidance not only from God but maybe even from a professional guidance counselor. However, if the two learn as much about one another as possible prior to getting married, a lot of their differences can be ironed out, or they may decide that there are too many irreconcilable differences to start a marriage. There maybe some difference that the two may never agree on, however, the couple must find some common ground or compromise. Between the two there must be an acceptance of each one's differences. If a man or woman cannot accept that the other thinks or feels differently about certain issues, then the union is in trouble. This is why it is so important that a couple receives prenuptial counseling. I hope this story helps to make my point clearer.

Once upon a time, Albert met Mary. As the relationship between the two begin to develop, neither of the two would address the other when he or she didn't agree with one another. Albert told Mary that he had a dream that they would have acquired enough in both their checking and saving account to live comfortably prior to having any children. This is plan that they are discussing prior to getting married. Mary asked well what if I get pregnant before we reach that goal? Albert replied by saying you'll just have to get an abortion, because the baby will come too soon. Mary eyes filled with water because she loved this man, but she was totally opposed to abortions. She went home that night trying to work it out in her mind how to deal with this. Well, she concluded that it would never be a situation in their marriage because she just will make sure that she doesn't get pregnant too soon. So as time went on they decided to become engaged. In the process of discussing the wedding, religion came up. Mary wanted a church wedding, but Albert's religion didn't allow him to go into a church. Again, they thought the best thing in this situation was just to have a yard wedding. It seems that they were compromising fairly well. However, their differences were becoming greater with less and less common ground. As they continue to ignore the great degree of differences, the relationship was becoming more estranged. However, they both were so good together, the chemistry was simply amazing that everything else was of a lesser priority. Mary kept convincing herself that this was the man of her dreams. She refused to hear anyone that tried to be objective about the relationship. No one could convince her that she was making a mistake. Albert on the other hand felt that Mary would always allow things to go how he had planned. He felt that the man was to be the head and the woman was to obey. Unfortunately, they did become husband and wife. As the marriage began to age, more and more difference began to surface. As usual Mary, would take down until one day she found herself in such a state of depression until she could hardly function. She felt all of herself had faded away. She felt that she was a different person from the visions she had of herself as a married woman.

After about six years of marriage, Albert decided he was ready to increase the size or their family. So Mary fell in line and became pregnant. Three children were added to this union, a set of twin boys and a little girl. She decided that once the children had reach preschool age that she would start taking them to church at her mother's church. Albert strongly expressed his disapproval. He said there was no way she was going to take his children up in that church because he didn't believe in that. He said they could go to his place of worship, which was not inside of a church. No he was not a devil worshipper, but he believed differently. Mary cried and cried, not knowing what to do. So the children didn't really get to go to any place of worship. As the children grew up, they would witness how estranged their parents were with one another. Mary continued in the marriage because she did not want to be viewed as a failure at marriage. Also, it was not in her religious belief to get divorced. Needless to say Mary became a very unhappy person. However, she was willing to accept all of Albert's commands and demands, until they began to affect his daughter. As a teenager, their daughter became pregnant and Albert decided without the benefit of counseling for his daughter, that she should have an abortion. The daughter as well as the mother felt very strongly that abortions were wrong. This is when Mary decided to tell Albert that she would not stand behind him on this decision. She told him if he could not accept their daughter and the grandchild that she and the children would leave. This began a battle. Albert had never compromised with Mary and he was not about to start. Mary took the children one day while he was at work and left for her mother's house. Albert called and threatened Mary with a court custody battle. He declared that he would get sole custody of the children. Mary felt dominated by Albert because that was the way their relationship had been developed from the beginning. So Mary and the children returned home and the daughter end up getting the abortion. Their daughter never emotionally recovered and needless to say Albert and Mary's marriage came to a devastating end. The children all grew up anxious to get out of that house where they witness so much unhappiness in their mother. After the children were out of the nest, Mary told Albert that it was over; that she felt imprisoned by the marriage and wanted out. That was the sad ending for Albert and Mary. Even though the man is the head and the wife is to obey according to King James Version of the Holy Bible, the two must be equally yoked, meaning they both have the same or similar beliefs and values about life and the issues they will encounter. In other words, the decision that the husband makes should not go totally against what the wife believes and feels. Some people view unequally-yoked as being a biracial couple, or one being of the Pentecostal religion and the other of the Baptist religion, however, it goes deeper than that. If two people coming from two totally different backgrounds find that in their hearts, they are more alike than different, a beautiful and successful marriage is possible for the two.

CAN WE BE DIFFERENT? AND BE SOUL MATES

Can we be different as two pieces of a puzzle but yet fit together?
Can we be different in color but blend in beauty as a bird's feathers?
Can we be different as the seasons, winter, spring summer and fall?
Each bringing in some bad as well as some good, but there's a purpose for them all.
Can we be different as the presence of the day and of the night,
Allowing the night to bring in the quiet of the darkness, and the day so bold and bright?
Can we be different in our perception of this life or what it should be,
Knowing that it is just what it is, without the opinions of either your or me?
Can we be different and yet one day discovers our missing part?
Can we be soul mates destine to meet and one day finds the other half of our heart?

Chapter Four

A LIFETIME OF COMPROMISE

Compromise according to *Webster Universal College Dictionary*, is defined as "a settlement of differences by mutual adjustment or modification of opposing claims, principles, demands, etc; agreement by mutual concession". Should a person compromise change him or her totally from the person he or she was? How far should the compromise go? Compromise is supposed to be an adjustment, not a makeover. It is virtually impossible to have a successful relationship without compromise. No one person within a relationship can have it his or her way all the time and not cause the relationship damage. However, it is important to know that a compromise is to find common ground, not to surrender all. In the last chapter it explained how two individual could be unequally yoked which makes a marriage virtually impossible. This chapter will explain how two individual can be different but come together. We've all heard the cliché "let's agree to disagree".

Let's look at that a little closer. How do two individual agree to disagree. First, each must recognize and respect the difference of opinion shared by the other individual. Second, the two must be open-minded in order to move forward, both agreeing that it is okay that the other doesn't feel the same way. Next, the two must come to an understanding of the common goal that is desired.

Finally both must be willing to give a little to reach that goal. Later in the chapter I will give an example of how two people can compromise.

Compromise misunderstood can become a total alteration in an individual character. If a person doesn't understand how compromise works, then he or she may very well give up who he or she is to make a relationship work. In this case the person has become compromised, meaning "unable to function optimally". (Webster Universal College Dictionary) Compromising and becoming compromised are two different things. Just as a compromised immune system, it is not serving its purpose. When an individual loses his or her purpose, he or she began to feel worthless. It is important to be able to give to a true meaningful relationship. If all that a person has to offer is never good enough or accepted by the other person, then there is no relationship. Why, because one of the individual has become useless in contributing to the relationship and it has become a one-man or a one-woman show. Eventually this type of relationship turns very bad. The compromised individual gets tired and will probably abort the relationship.

Once the couple has realized that they disagree on an issue, the two can agree that there is a conflict, but are willing to seek a common goal to settle their differences. The second step will be for each person to accept and respect the feelings of the other person. This is very important in trying to find a common ground. Each person in the relationship must be willing to objectively listen to what the other person is saying and to respect that person's strong feeling about the situation. If the two really wants the relationship to work, then this is where compromise steps in. Both must realize that it will not turn out exactly how each of them would desire for it to be, but that they can both get some of their wishes with a compromise. Hopefully, in this short story about Jake and Amber, the reader will get a clearer picture of true compromise.

Jake and Amber have been married for almost two years. At first they were living in an apartment, but decided that it would be wise to purchase their own home. Well, they both went house shopping. Both had different ideals about what would be a good investment for their first home. Amber wanted to get a house that was small and cozy, while Jake thought that they should think ahead and get a house that would be big enough to accommodate their future increase in family size. They both sat down and discussed their family planning goals. They decided that they would like to start having children in approximately three more years. Amber agreed that maybe they should look for something a little bigger and convert to something even bigger as the family grows; and Jake agreed that buying a smaller house than what he had originally wanted would be more feasible for their current income and family size. This was a great example of compromise.

Once Jake and Amber settled into their new home, they decided to start looking at other goals that they wanted for themselves. They discussed careers, children, budgets, and all that good stuff. Amber said that she would like to continue to work as a Registered Nurse and take some night course in hope to one day become a nurse practitioner. Jake was pretty much satisfied with his job in construction. He had a distance dream of one day owning his own construction company, but no short-term goals at this time of pursuing that dream.

After about two and a half years, Amber became pregnant. She was in her first trimester of pregnancy and her third semester of college. Jake decided that she should quit school for a while and stay home with the baby until he or she reaches preschool age. Amber did not want to put her life on hold, but wanted to hire a nanny for the baby. Jake said that was out of the question. He was not willing to compromise and Amber had to put her dreams on hold. Well that was the first piece of Amber that she lost. Two years later she became pregnant again. With the same rule applying for this child, that was another three to four years that she was on hold. After the second child became preschool age, and Amber was getting ready to get back in school, Jake decided that he wanted to pursue his dream and start his own construction company. Upon discussing it, he explained to Amber why they could not afford for her to go to school right now, because of his new business adventure. He again would not listen to what she was feeling. He told her what the deal was and she didn't try and fight it. Well needless to say years passed by and Amber never did complete her goal in becoming the nurse practitioner that she so desired. As time went on she just allowed Jake to make all the decisions and she just went alone. She became very distance and agitated. She was short with the children and less optimistic about life. Over the years, Amber had loss the person that she was and became the person that lived her husband's dreams, and not the dreams of a happily married couple.

Remember, don't lose who you are to the person you love. But if you are true to whom you are and add the right amount of compromise, a beautiful and prosperous marriage can be your prize.

True Compromise

I listen to what you are thinking and I respect what you feel,
And I expect you to do the same for me so we can keep it real.
No more twain, but we've become as one, joined by God above,
Only if we're together in body and soul sealed by his love.
Can you accept me, for who I am, as I convert to who we are,
As I give you room to meet me halfway and not expect you to come too far?
It's been said the soul of a man is seen through his eyes,
So face to face, staring into each other's soul, we can find true compromise.

Chapter Five

What is a Commitment

What is a commitment? According to Webster's College Dictionary, it is the act of being committed. To Commit according to the same source is "to give in trust or charge, to cosign". What does commitment mean to a successful marriage? One must be willing to commit to another person in order to have a good relationship. An individual cannot partially commit to a relationship as serious as a marriage. Once you promise that other individual that you will be his or her lifetime partner that comes with total commitment. Committing to a marriage is more than committing to a friendship, a job, or a weight-loss program. All of the others cost a person much less to renege on than breaking a marriage vow. So before you commit decide if you are willing to fully commit. A relationship will become one-sided if both people are not willing to fully commit.

Commitment involves giving up some of the things that's done as a single person. It's a lifetime of sharing in bad times as well as good times. Many people do not realize that when they commit to those marriage vows to stick with another individual for better or worse, for richer or poorer, in sickness and in health until death do them part, is a very serious commitment. It doesn't mean leaving the person because he or she loses his or her job. Neither does it mean turning to a life of infidelity if the other person loses the physical beauty or attraction that he or she once possessed. Committing to another person in a marriage is life altering and takes lots of conscious effort. A person must realize that what he or she does will affect their spouse.

If your mate had a problem committing prior to marriage, chances are great that that person will have that same problem once the two of you are married. So many couples proceed with the nuptials hoping that legalizing the relationship will make their mate become faithful and committed. Most of the times the mate that has practice being unfaithful, will continue to do so after marriage, because he or she assumes that you know what he or she is all about and have accepted it. Infidelity, one of the leading causes of the increase in divorce rate, will not be solved by jumping the broom. An individual must free his or her self from practicing such a behavior. An individual must be faithful to him/herself first before he or she can be faithful to another. Having to jump from partner to partner is an inner issue that an individual person must seek help to find out why he or she cannot commit to just one person.

Infidelity is a problem that is ignored and denied in many marriages. Mostly the women will acted as though it is not true expecting it to just go away. Sometimes everyone in the surrounding area will be talking about how someone is cheating on his or her spouse and the spouse seems to know nothing of the such, or just simply chooses to not believe that it is true.

Infidelity is a very serious violation of the sacred vows of a marriage. Some women have made the comment as long as he is coming home to momma and bringing me the money I don't care about those women out there.

Some will say, but I love him and having a piece of man is better than no man at all. But, there can be detrimental consequences to accepting a spouse to continue to sleep around. There are so many STDs that are incurable and can cause an innocent person as that accepting spouse his or her life. So I am not encouraging anyone to leave his or her spouse because he or she is not faithful, however I urge you if you are going to stay there to be very careful with intimate relations. One must seek God as to whether or not this marriage can be repaired. Do my mate and I have enough sincere qualities as a couple to make this marriage work?

Through listening at conversations of others, I've learned that people believe and try to convince others that one spouse is responsible for the other spouse infidelity. The argument is that the cheating spouse is looked at as the bad spouse and the other spouse is looked at as the victim. These people go on to say that the cheating spouse is justified in cheating, because he or she has a need or needs that his or her spouse is not meeting. I beg to differ, it is time that we all stand up and accept responsibility for our own actions and not place blame at no one else feet. This is why communication is so essential to a marriage. If one spouse feels so strongly about that need that's not being met, then he or she to sit down and talk to the other spouse until an understanding is reached. In other words there is no justification for infidelity. Even if a person make the mistake of cheating because of a heated moment that arose because that outside man or woman could feel what the spouse need, this does not have to become a lasting affair. If one truly honors the vows he or she made to God and his or her mate, then he or she will quickly correct his or her action.

This book has mostly addressed those who are considering getting married. I haven't said much to those couples who are already married, but not sure if that was the right move or if the person they married is truly their soul mate. Don't feel alone. There are many marriages in trouble. It is the job of the devil, an enemy to us all, to try and destroy the family structure. However, if there is confusion as to whether or not you should stay married to your current spouse, then you need to seek guidance from God. You should do as I've stressed to those who haven't yet married and be certain first of all as to who you are and what you want. Are you willing to commit to this marriage? There indeed must be a commitment in order for your marriage to work, but the commitment must be shared by both individuals in the marriage. What if you don't know where the other person stands on commitment? Well, this is an opportunity for you to practice your communication skills. Talk to your spouse. Even if he or she doesn't seem to be interested in having a conversation about his or her willingness to commit, you must still open up the lines of communication that you will know if your spouse are aware of what you are feeling. Remember as I've already said in this book you must be true to yourself before you can be true to your spouse.

I've seen so many marriages where one spouse lives to please the other with no true regard to his or her own feelings and beliefs. There must be true compromise, but it must be shared in order for one spouse not to lose who he or she truly is to the other spouse. A marriage is only working when it is a partnership. If one spouse is bending over backward to please the other and the other is putting forth no efforts, then the marriage is not going to be successful. Marriages of this nature have survived over the years, but that spouse that constantly did all the giving, basically lived a long miserable and unhappy life. It is not God's will that we live this way, for it is his will that we have life and have it more abundantly.

Okay, I know you maybe thinking well what do I do. I am not sure of anything about my marriage. My spouse is being very difficult and I am getting frustrate. First of all you need to step back for a minute and talk to God. You must pray for your marriage and for your spouse. Please know that even though you may pray, God will not force that spouse to do nothing he or she doesn't want to do. Yet you can still have faith that if you pray for him or her, that God will grant your request and that spouse will become enlighten and his or her understanding will be open up concerning the marriage. See sometimes, your spouse might not truly know what his or her actions are doing to you or the marriage. Regardless of how hard you try to get him or her to see. This is why you need a relationship with God. I will even suggest that some seek marital counseling. If you cannot get the spouse to participate, some individual counseling may help you to understand what you want to do about your current situation.

There are so many opinions out there waiting to flood your ears about what you should do about your marriage and the rationale for those opinions. Some are backed by religious belief, some by experience that others have had in their own marriages, and some biased by relations to either you or your spouse. However, every individual marriage is different, what may have worked for my marriage, doesn't necessarily means it will work for your marriage. So you must seek God for your answers. I am not telling you not to listen to no one else, but I am telling you to listen to God. If he speaks to you through someone else, you will know that it is him speaking because you have been praying and seeking answers of him.

Marriage is indeed a sacred union and a very serious one. If it is not viewed as been sacred and serious by both individual, you have a problem. We should let our marriage be a model marriage for our children. We should be able to show them how to love and respect their spouse. Let's be careful not to live a life before our children of hell and abuse. Understand that I am no way telling you to leave your spouse, nor am I telling you to stay with him or her, but I will say whatever decision you make let it be good for all parties involved, including you, your spouse, and your children.

Many people have stayed in a marriage because others have told them divorce is wrong according to God. The bible in the book of Matthew the 19th chapter, the ninth verse said "and I say unto you, whosoever shall put away his wife, except it be for fornication, and marry another, committed adultery; and who so married her which is put away, doth commit adultery". (*Authorized King James Version copyright 1994)* In this passage of scripture Jesus was speaking to the disciples on the law that Moses had made concerning divorce. I will say unto you that getting a divorce is as serious as getting married. It should not be taken lightly and that you should seek God concerning such a move. I cannot encourage anyone to stay in a situation that will jeopardize your life and well being. If you have an abusive spouse or a habitual adulterer, then you definitely need to seek God for you answers immediately. I know of people who have stayed in marriages because of religion or other strong belief and have lost their life to physical abuse from the other spouse. Some have stayed with the notion if I do right, regardless of what my spouse does God will protect me, and those people have gotten incurable diseases from that spouse, that have cause them a lot of physical, not to mention psychological pain. So seek God for your answer. God is just and he knows your heart. He also knows the heart of your spouse. He knows if your spouse will ever love you, as he should. So if you married this person without first acknowledging God, it's not too late to acknowledge him now. Of course pray for you spouse and you marriage. Ask God to help him or her to have a change of mind concerning the marriage. For there are some that have married another for many reasons, and love not being one of them. Yet, by the power of prayer from the other spouse, that uncommitted spouse turned from his or her ways and through God their marriage became very successful and fulfilling. Yes, the bible did say a sanctified wife, could sanctify the husband, if he believes. So it's not what I say or what others say, but what God says. Remember he might say it through the voice of others, but pray that their voice will be a confirmation of what God has already told you in your heart.

Who will Truly Lose

When I chose you as my mate, I promised to be with you and only you.
I vowed before God and man that I would honor you and to be true.

If for some reason due to weakness, I slip and break that vow,
I must diligently work to correct it and to make it right somehow.

I mustn't take our sacred union lightly, but instead give it the ultimate respect,
And cherish you as my soul mate and other half, just as God expects.

I must honor my commitment to the marriage and stay within the boundaries set for you and me.
And when temptation invites me to step away, I must remind myself where I should be.

I must truly consider the commitment made when marriage is what I choose,
For if I violate those vows made before God and Man, who will truly lose?

Know this, that infidelity is not the only way that a person can be unfaithful. If at any given time in the marriage, a spouse reneges on his or her responsibilities that is an unfaithful act. If the wife neglects her wifely duties, she is unfaithful. If she decides that she will not be intimate with her spouse as punishment because he will not give her what she wants, she is being unfaithful. If a man vows to take care of his wife and decides that he doesn't want to work and provide for her anymore, he is being unfaithful. Being faithful is sticking to the vows that you made to one another before men and God. Being faithful to a marriage means more than just not cheating, but it also means consciously remembering what you vowed to do when you two became husband and wife.

If a couple decides to enlarge their family by having children, they must be willing to commit themselves as parents. This will mean losing some more personal time and space. It is not a picture book fairytale; it is a reality. Just because two people decide that they want to start a family and are not prepared to commit, doesn't set the foundation for a happy and successful life for the parents or the children.

It is a common fact that men are less apt to make a commitment than a woman. It takes a man much longer to prepare himself to commit to one woman. A man also considers the fact that once he commits to a marriage, he is taking the greater responsibility. He realizes that he is the one that is solely responsible for providing for that family. Why, because of the belief that a man is the head of his house lays that responsibility not only in his lap, but also heavily on his mind. It is understandable that women become weary of men who procrastinate on making a commitment. However, it is good that they don't commit if they're not ready to do so. Yes, sometime women force a man into commitment by giving him an ultimatum to commit or move on. Then when the two gets into the marriage and the man cheats or fail in his responsibility, the woman seems baffled and upset. Well, it was obvious that the man was not ready for a true commitment, but he committed solely to satisfy the woman. So women, be aware of a man's reservation about committing and take into consideration the long term effect that it will have on your marriage.

Another, commitment, that has been made by women, that they did not want to do, is cohabitation. There are many women living in what's called a common-law-marriage, because the man was not willing to commit to a legal marriage. Again, the woman shouldn't want the man to commit if he is not ready, however, the woman should not commit to living in a cohabitated relationship if that is not what she really wants. Sometime women commit to that kind of relationship believing that the men will one day come to their senses and marry them. Most of the time, this is not the case. There is an old cliché that states "why buy the cow, when you get the milk free". So it is important that a person is ready and prepared to commit, prior to doing so. No marriage or relationship will be successful if both individual is not willing to fully commit.

When a couple gets married, there is another commitment that they make; and it is to God. Many people do not consider this when they take this step. The couple stands before God and man and vow to commit their lives to one another. They are also taking that sacred oath to stick with that one individual until death do them part. Yet when things get tough, most people don't think twice when reneging on that commitment to the spouse or to God. This is why it is vitally important that the individuals seek guidance, counseling, and approval prior to getting married. Guidance and counseling from an objective professional, whether it is a man or woman of God, or whether it a professional counselor. Finally, the couple should seek approval from the God in each individual own life, "*God did you send this mate to me*".

Chapter Six

Factors To Consider When Choosing a Mate

Are there things that should be considered when choosing a mate? Yes, an individual should know as much about their potential spouse as possible. Why, because the more that person knows, the easier the decision to marry or not will be. What are some of the things that a person should consider researching about their potential spouse? Learn something about the person background and or history, something about his or her race/ethnicity, about his or her financial status, something about their health, and something about their religious or general belief. These factors will be helpful in not only deciding the compatibility as a couple, but the likelihood of having healthy and happy children.

Looking into a person background prior to marriage can be helpful in understanding why that person does several things the way he or she does them. Hopefully there is nothing from one's background that he or she can't trust their potential spouse with. If it is a legal issues even something as serious as murder, to something as minor as a poor credit history, both issues, if concealed, can cause a problem when the two become husband and wife. This information does not have to include petty things such as how many boyfriends or girlfriends the other has had, but if something significant about one of those boyfriends or girlfriends will affect the marriage, it needs to be revealed. If a person has an incurable venereal disease, that is an important factor to share with a potential spouse. If a person is transgender that is something that a potential spouse needs to know. I know that it is a person privilege to keep such information private. However, if information of such serious nature as fore mention becomes uncovered by the other spouse, it can cause irreversible damage to the marriage. If a person knows the worse thing about his potential mate and can still love that person and share a life with that person, there is little or no doubt about the sincerity of love of that person. However shallow it may seem, if learning something from another person's background will cause the other person to love him or her less, then, a marriage is not the best thing for this couple at the presence time. Not saying that these two people would automatically fail at a marriage, however, someone should strongly encourage them to take more time to know each other, and to definitely seek prenuptial counseling.

Race and ethnicity are also factors that should be taken into consideration. One might wonder what is the difference in the two? According to Webster's Universal College Dictionary, race is a group of persons related by common descent or heredity; and ethnicity is ethnic traits, background allegiance, or association. So either of the two represents where a person comes from, whether it is by heredity or association.

Yes, I know love has no color, but the hearts and minds of many people do. It is possible for and individual to become so physically attracted to another, that one individual will deeply burry his or her true feeling about the race or ethnicity of the potential spouse. However, the situation can become more complicated when marriage is brought to the table. Why, because marriage brings in other relatives from the sides of both individuals. Because the individual who has buried his or her true feelings about that particular race or ethnic background, it becomes difficult for him or her to accept the relatives of his or her future spouse. The individual feels no physical attraction for the relatives, therefore making it impossible for he or she to camouflage what is really there.

Statistical facts tell us that financial hardship is one of the leading causes of divorce today. Looking in to the financial status of a potential spouse would be wise to avoid later surprises. Not that it should be a major factor in deciding whether or not one will marry that individual, but at least it will give insight on what a person will be working with. It will be a rude awakening if one individual who has worked so diligently to keep his or her credit in good standing and marries an individual who has very poor credit. Yes, the credit of one spouse can be vastly affected by the action of the other spouse. Even though one spouse can apply for things in his or her name only, eventually it will become intertwined because of various reasons such as needing both spouses income. Later in this chapter, there will be a short story to reiterate these facts.

There are also cases where one individual is not being honest with the other about his or her financial status in order to make a good impression. For instance a man might lead his lady friend to think that he has more than he really does. Why, because men know that a woman is looking for someone who is able and willing to take care of her. Even, though many women are defined as liberal and independent, they still want a financial stable and capable man. Women have also been known to hide things from their financial background, such as all those credit cards that are maximized because they had to look beautiful. So why go into marriage with a factor hanging over ones head that will lead to divorce. Nothing is impossible if God ordains it, but make certain that he did.

Why would it be necessary for a person to seek answers from their potential mate about his or her medical background? If two people become married and wants to start a family, it is good to know the medical history of each other. When comparing these histories, the two can be aware of what potential traits that they are both carrying and how it can affect their children if they decide to have any. It is also good to know the potential long-term problems that might occur over the years.

Finally, it is important to know about the religious or general beliefs of one's potential spouse. This is a factor that can definitely determine if the two individuals are unequally yoked or not. Two people must be able to agree on the major issues in life in order to have a successful marriage. If one person believes in God and the other one does not, then as a couple, there will be a problem. So many of times, during the courting stage and even the engagement period, a couple will avoid addressing such uncomfortable issues as religion and finances. However, it is an issue that will eventually come to surface and can cause some major problems. Hopefully this short story will shed some light as to the importance of disclosing one another's past.

Let's call this couple Jack and Jill. When Jack and Jill met, the chemistry and physical attraction was amazing. They hit it off immediately. They had nice conversations and great dates. They commented each other all the time. Jill was biracial and Jack was an African-American.

The two decided that they were a perfect match and began planning their wedding. Of course Jack allowed Jill to make all the arrangements for the wedding as she so desired. Needless to say, Jack's relatives had very little input on this wedding. During the actual ceremony, some of Jack's relatives began to openly criticize the choice of food that was chosen by Jill's family for the reception. Jill was a descendant of an African-American father and a Caucasian mother. However, her Caucasian relatives reared her. So her family side at the ceremony was predominately white and Jack's side of course was all black. This of course did very little in making this wedding ceremony go smoothly. Well, they got married and started their lives together. As time past and they decided to buy a house, Jill learned that Jack had previously filed bankruptcy just two years ago. He had a very good income but terrible credit, and on the other hand, she had good credit, but only worked as a receptionist with not much income. So she wanted to ask her mother and stepfather to co-sign for them to get their first mortgage. They were reluctant, because of his history of making payments and his bad credit. Jill became very upset with Jack for not telling her that before they got married. He responded by saying "oh if you knew that I had filed bankruptcy, then you would not have married me". Jill said, "I don't know". This was the beginning of the end. As time went on the two of them discovered more and more about each other's background and it was more than the chemistry and physical attraction could handle. After only 18 months of marriage, Jill had filed for divorce.

Chapter Seven

The Combination to a Successful Marriage

It is important that a person understands his or her own self prior to trying to understand someone else. What does that mean, to know one's own self? Well, many people don't realize their true inner self as well as they should, simply because they have not studied it well enough. Many people try to live pleasing to others and forget to see if that is what they really feel to be right for them. There is pressure from parents, from friends, from the Church, and from society in general. Why do we listen so hard to what other tells us about ourselves as opposed to listening to our heart and inner man. Some people don't realize that they are doing this until they're almost middle age adults. Yes, there are those small percent that figure this out as young adults and even a few as a teenager.

However, an individual must become acquainted with who he or she really is, and what he or she really wants. One should know his or her true beliefs about life and life issues that one will be faced with. People are so quick to give advice and opinions. The advice of others doesn't always be the answer for each individual person. What may work for one very well may not work for the other. If a person searches and researches his or her most inner being, he or she will find that there are things about his or her self that they hadn't realized. In the midst of studying one's own beliefs and feelings, a person can began to understand how he or she responds to the action and behaviors of others. Is the response a sincere and honest response or is it a practical one designed by the rules and opinions of others? As long as a person continues to be untrue to his or her self, then he or she can never be true to someone else. In other words if one goes into a marriage with unresolved issues it will inevitably spill over into the marriage. So many people not knowing what he or she really wants, makes the mistake of thinking another person can fill that void. However, each individual must be a complete soul, before the two can become a whole. A person's soul mate will only make the other complete when both are assured of their own belief. This is an important part of preparing to be a spouse. This is why so many people in broken marriages blame the other spouse for the mistake the he or she makes. If a person is not true to his or her self, than he or she will not understand how to resolve inner conflict and certainly not conflict with another. What is inner conflict? Inner conflict is when a person does not know what is or is not right for him or her. Once an individual knows his or her self, being in a relationship is much easier. Knowing ones own true feelings helps a person to separate what he or she wants from what he thinks the other person expects him or her to want. One must be careful to be truthful about how he or she feels early in the relationship. If a person always responds to please his or her mate, then chances of true compromise will be little to none. It is important that an honest response is there for both individuals in order to learn about the other person's belief. As the couple began to learn about each other, dishonesty will camouflage symptoms of future problems within the marriage. It is virtually impossible to learn about each other if both are not honest with each other. For instance, if one tells the other that he doesn't believe in interracial relationships, and the other person claims to share mutual beliefs but really doesn't, that is the beginning of a dishonest relationship. The person that was dishonest is not being true to herself neither her mate. An individual cannot be fearful of being honest and true to his or her self or his or her mate.

You Must Be True to Yourself To be Honest With Me!

If you ask me how I feel, can you handle what I Might say,
Or will you be expecting me to respond, by seeing things your way?

If you ask me what I think, are your mind opened enough to hear,
Or will your perception be tainted by what you think, simply because of fear?

If you opened up your mind and ask me, is the truth what I will speak,
Or, will my response be what I think you want, because I am too weak?

If you gave me the chance, would I be true to myself,
Or will my answers be based on the belief, of someone else?

Can we speak to each other from our heart, being confident in our own belief,
Or will we live in fear of the other's response, and continue existing in deceit?

Communication is definitely a vital part of the combination for a successful marriage. What is communication? To communicate according to *Webster's Universal College Dictionary* is "to impart knowledge of; make known; divulge". Everyday people attempt to communicate to one another. However, all communication is not effective communication. Simply talking to each other doesn't necessarily mean that communication was effective. The dictionary defined the word communication as to make known. Sometimes when people talk, the speaker is saying one thing and the listener perceives something totally different. Somehow the lines of communication became scrambled.

There are three things one must do to communicate effectively. One must be an active listener, seek clarification, and give feedback. If those three components are not presence then the parties involved may give and receive information with an entirely different understanding. The conception and perception may not intertwine.

How can a person be an active listener? He or she must give and receive eye contact and observe for the use and to use body gestures and nonverbal communication. Nonverbal communication also lets the parties involve better understand each other. It helps the speaker to watch the body gestures of his or her audience to see if they are bored or interested in what is being said. It helps the listener to watch the body gestures of the speaker because it reiterates what is being said. If a person practices those things, then he or she will be giving his or her full attention during the course of communicating.

Seeking clarification will also help in avoiding communication errors. Sometime by simply restating what one just heard will allow the person speaking, to know that he or she understood what was said. Asking questions is another way to seek clarity. Ask the person to elaborate more on something that may not be as clear as one may need it to be.

The third one was to give feedback. Even if a person thought that he or she did perceive the concept that was intended, giving feedback would let the speaker know if a miscommunication had occurred. Miscommunication is a simple mix up in message given and message received. So if the person doesn't use the first two methods, feedback will help to unscramble the lines of communication.

So one can see how communication is very important to a marriage. The couple must be able to communicate in order to stay together. Not addressing something will not make it go away. It may burry it for a little while, but the problem will still be there. Many couples avoid communicating because it is not always a pleasant exercise. As the couple began to communicate, some emotions can surface and some feeling can be hurt. Communicating, however, unpleasant is the main key to resolving any problems in a marriage. However, both people in the marriage must listen, and seek understanding of what the other person is saying. Both individuals in the marriage must realize that however, wrong one or the other might be, it must be communicated in order for the person to see the error and correct it. If communication is lost in a marriage, it will either end or become a very difficult relationship to continue.

The final part to the combination of a successful marriage is to seek God's stamp of approval. One must acknowledge God in all his or her ways and lean not unto his or her own understanding. One must pray to God to show him or her the true person that he or she is about to vow to spend the rest of his or her life with. A person must also seek God's guidance as to whether or not he or she is ready to be a husband or wife. How will one know if God approves. This will depend on the kind of relationship that an individual share with God. The person might be able to get his or her answer directly from God, through prayer and communication with God. Others may need more counseling from a higher official in his or her church or religious organization. Regardless of how much the two as a couple might seem to have it going on, without the ordinance of God, the marriage has a high risk of failure. God needs to be apart of your marriage. He should be consulted often, even daily if possible to help the marriage to stay alive and prosperous.

If perhaps you are already in a marriage, but not sure if you should stay in it or leave it, you too needs to consult God. Sometimes a marriage can be suffering because some of the components such as those mentioned in this book are missing. Well, God can place that resource in your life to help you and your mate to find the missing parts. However, both parties must be willing to seek an answer from God. If in the case that the two of you married unequally yoked, and your differences are too great that they are irreconcilable, a divorce maybe the only answer. However, seek God prior to ending the marriage, the answer is in God.

The Conclusion of The Matter

(Based on a true story)

Millie and Jim met over twenty years ago. At first, their relationship seemed to be one of a short nature. Neither one of them ever thought the other one was their soul mate. The two dated off and on for over seven years. A daughter was born, that bonded the two people for life. Even though the physical attraction and chemistry was not all that, the two could always talk openly with the other and enjoyed being friends. Honesty was also a strong attribute of this relationship. Because of the honest nature, neither one ever expected any more than what the other person said that he or she had to offer. Understand that even though a child was born out of wedlock, the two did not marry just because the child was born. For the two knew that would not be enough to base a life-time of commitment on. They remain friends and both played and active role as parent in the child's life.

Of course over the years, the relationship became one-sided. Millie fell in love with Jim, but he didn't return the feelings. He remained honest with Millie and did not say the four-letter word LOVE, until he actually meant it. Millie began to suffer more hurt in the relationship, because she now needed more, than Jim was willing to give. As time went on Jim began to realize that Millie would do almost anything for him, so unconsciously he took advantage of the situation and would go and come as he pleased within the relationship. Yes, as many people have done, when he found out that Millie really loved him and needed him, he took for granted that regardless of what he does, she would always be there. Sorry once you fall in love, you cannot tell your heart not to love. So many times those that are in love do foolish things. These things are especially foolish to those on the outside looking in.

After years of being broken hearted and seeing many disappointments, Millie decided to go to God. She prayed that God would allow Jim to move on and leave her alone. Well, for a little while, she began to believe that God had granted her request. Jim began a relationship with one of Millie's friend girls from her past. Millie felt that was the last straw and that would help her close the book on Jim and Millie. Even though their relationship had ended, Jim continued to come around to see his daughter. Millie became very involved in the church and had accepted that she would live the rest of her life as a celibate single mother. She seemed very content in the church and was not looking nor praying for God to send her a husband.

Well after two years, Jim reappeared. His relationship with Millie's friend girl had ended. Of course Millie told Jim that she was no longer interested in anything that he had to say about a relationship between the two. She said that he was welcome to spend as much time with their daughter as he would like. However, Jim was persistence in trying again to pursue Millie. Millie was proud of the fact that she was able to resist his efforts regardless of how charmed and sincere they seemed.

A tragic incidence occurred in Millie's extended family. Millie was grief-stricken and Jim was there to support her. She really needed his friendship at the time. Well, the storm blew over, and Millie discovered that she was back in that old rut. She became angry and question God as to how he allow this man back into her life, when she had made such great progress in moving on with her life. She could not understand how God would allow her to go through such pain and agony again. Now what was Millie to do? Here she was in love again with this rascal, and he could care less about her, she thought. So after Millie come to accept that she had once again fallen into Jim's trap, she began to seek God for some help. She prayed and asked God to define the relationship between her and Jim. She sought God for a direct answer, as to whether Jim was her husband or not. She was determined to keep her relationship with God, which did not include a life of fornication between her and Jim. So she went on a fast and asked God to allow Jim to propose to her on his next visit if he was her husband. She was truly not expecting this proposal being that Jim had strongly expressed in the past that he had no intentions of getting married and he still had not yet ever told Millie that he loved her. Well two weeks later, Jim came to see Millie. He had been drinking alcohol as usual. He did propose to Millie three times that night. Still in denial, showing a tremendous lack of faith, Millie charged it to the alcohol and the fact that Jim knew that she was weary about their relationship and was thinking of ending it. When Jim returned on another day and revisited the conversation about marriage, Millie told him that he had never told her that he loved her. He explained that he hadn't because of his inability to express the way he felt, but that he did love her dearly. Millie was astonished at the fact that God had answered her prayer requested yet she lacked the faith and patience to wait on God to finish what he had started. Millie became so excited and asked Jim to move in with her, acting against everything she was taught and knew to be right, what a mistake she made.

Millie and Jim began cohabitating. This arrangement lasted for over a year. Millie would go to church, sit, and cry the whole entire time she was there. Living in sin and regret, she did not possess the strength or power to put him out. She would leave church and make promises to herself that when she got home, she would give him the ultimatum to do the right thing and marry her or to move out. Upon such discussion, Jim would always find an excuse as to why it just wasn't the right time. She would still commit the sinful act and cry herself to sleep. Well, Millie wised up one day and realized that this problem was too much for her to solve. Even though she believed that Jim was indeed her husband, she realized that she had messed up by inviting him to drink the milk, before he brought the cow. So she began to pray to God, asking him to get her out of a mess that she herself had created. She begged God to make Jim step up and do the right thing. As time passed, Jim continued to procrastinate. One day Millie stood in a prayer line and made a monetary sacrifice. The Prophet told all that were in the line that because of the sacrifice, a financial miracle was headed their way. Even though Millie needing a financial miracle too, she requested that God would grant her back a true relationship with him instead, one free of sin and her live-in-boyfriend. She told God, if I don't have the strength to tell him to leave, please do it for me. Millie was so torn between her love for God and her love for Jim, however, she decided that night, that she wanted her relationship with God more than her relationship with Jim. She knew that she had to put God first. So she just knew it was over between her and Jim. When Millie returned home on that night after church, she went to Jim and looked him in the eye, prepared to ask him to leave. Jim told her before she could say one word, that they would get married the following Saturday, only six days away, they became husband and wife.

Jim was afraid to commit, because he didn't know if he could be the husband that he thought Millie deserve. He did not know if he would be able to provide for his family. This was going into a foreign land for him and the very thought frightened him. Well, eventually he bit the bullet and stepped out on faith. For sixteen years Jim and Millie have been happily married. They have two beautiful children and a God filled life. Marriage of course did not solve all the problems that the two would have to face. Jim was not that man after God's own heart. He was not living a life pleasing unto God. However, Millie still felt that they were equally-yoked, because they both had such similar beliefs of how they wanted their lives to be. Jim had several habits including the strong hold of alcohol that had consumed his life. Jim has overcome his habits and given his life to God also. Jim was told by the doctor that he would die because of his drinking. He became very ill. Millie pleaded with Jim to stop the drinking. She even tried to convince him to stop by using their newborn son. She told him that Jim, Jr. would need him and if he couldn't stop drinking for himself, he should consider doing it for his son and his daughter. He went to the doctors and got medicine to help with the withdrawal symptoms, as he would try to stop. Nothing seemed to work. He just could not stop. Millie had cried and prayed consistently for months. Again, she turned to God and gave it to him. She began to pray for God to help her to accept whatever would come her way. Jim began his relationship with God by praying for himself, asking God to remove the desire to drink from him. He had went on another doctor visit and on his walk back to his home, he told God that he had one beer left in the refrigerator and that when he drank that beer, he would never drink another, and he hasn't. Amazingly the withdrawals symptoms was so minor, it was as though he had none. He has been sober for over thirteen years and is serving in his local church.

They have had some ups and downs within their marriage, but the two continued to communicate as husband and wife as they did as friends prior to the marriage. They realized that they had to have God as the head of their union; so that when things that seemed too big for the two of them, they could consult God having faith, that he would lead and guide them to the right solution. The two still consider themselves to be each other's best friend. No, there aren't any perfect marriages, but so far Jim and Millie have had a very successful one. So far there haven't been any serious fights or breakups between the two. There have been some serious issues that developed during the first decade of the marriage, but the two were able to communicate and to resolve the issues. Even though their marriage has not been perfect, the two feel that it has been a blessing. They both thank God daily for such a beautiful union that he has given to them. There have been some trials that they have had to overcome. Yet they loved each other enough to work through them.

Outside people will try to intervene into a marriage; especially if they think that the two people are doing well and that they might be happy. These people don't know really what's going on behind close doors, yet they will try to intrude if possible. Wives be aware of those women that envy wives of husband that do not cheat. Yes many will try your husband. Yes, I agree that the men must be strong and must resist temptation, however, be careful to whom you share private details with about your marriage. Some people set out to break up other people happy home because of pure jealousy. Single women, be conscious of the things that you do with married men. For the bible tells us "God is not mocked whatsoever a man sow, that shall he also reap". (Galatians 6:7 of the King James Version). So if you cheat with someone's husband, you can expect someone to cheat you out of a couple of nights with your husband, or even a lasting affair. Married men, be careful not to lose what you already have, by looking for greener pasture. Single men, as to single women, if they are spoken for leave them alone. Men know how hard it is for them to take a betrayal by a woman. Men have lost out on a life time with their soul mate, simply because they were unable to forgive that woman for one mistake.

Jim and Millie are working together to understand each other and growing closer everyday because of their efforts. They have decided that they are partners for life. Although Jim is the head of his house, that doesn't decrease the respect he has for his wife. He doesn't always agree with her, but he values her opinion and respects her feeling. Likewise, Millie respects her husband as head of the house. She listens to what he feels and doesn't always agree, however, compromise is a strong attribute in this marriage. The two have learned to not speak in anger. If anger creeps in they will take a break until they cool down. They are careful not to throw accusations or place blame. They remind each other that they both want the same goals in life.

Jim and Millie really enjoy each other's company. So much so, that they have difficulty sharing their time with other people. They like to laugh and spend quality time with one another. They work well together in the financial aspect of their marriage. It's gets rocky sometime when making decisions concerning their eighteen-year-old daughter. Yet they seem to figure it out somehow. In this case a whole lot of compromising is needed.

Marriage takes a lot of hard work, from both individuals. It takes more than physical attraction, money, and children to make a marriage work. Some marriages are still existing, but not working for both individual. Some people feel force to stay in a relationship for various reasons, none of them being love. Some stay because of their strong religious belief against divorce, some because of the children, and some because they feel they have nowhere else to go and are financially dependent on their spouse.

I've witness some marriage that I would not like my marriage to patterned after. I've seen women suffer in marriages and be so unhappy. This is a curse that I would like to see end. This is why I was inspired by God to write this book, that couples everywhere will seek guidance and counseling prior to taking such a tremendous step. There are resources available for people both engaged and already married to help them work through difficulties they might be facing. Remember seek God as to your answer. Not that they will come directly from God as with Jim and Millie, but that he will send the answer in, how he sees fit, or how he knows you will best receive it. Let your marriage be inspired by LOVE and ordain by GOD.

This book was written in 2008, almost four years ago. An update on Jim and Millie, they are still going strong as it appears to me.

Inspiration and Dedication

This book was inspired by the understanding and wisdom of God from within me. Many people that I am acquainted with have told me that I needed to use my talent. I know that those people wanted me to use what God gave me to get some of the things that I need. However, I must admit, that it was My Aunt Gloria, who called me one morning and told me that God spoke to her and told her to tell me that it is time for me to write the book. It's has been some months since I received that called, however, I began immediately seeking God as to what to write. I love to write poetry, but God put this book in my heart. I would like to dedicate this book to my love, my partner, and my Soul Mate, Mr. Anthony Bolton along with my two beautiful children, Chasity and Anthony Jr.

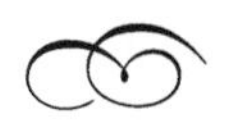

I am only a vessel of God, sent to do his will. I am not a person who enjoys being spotlighted. It was difficult for me to take the step to write this book, because I did not want to be shown publicly or drawn out before others, but also because I simply felt that no one wanted to hear what I had to say. Well, they won't hear what I have to say, for every word in this book was inspired by the Spirit of God that lives within me. As I sit to write this book, I took no premeditated thoughts, nor did I have to sit and plunder what to write. I simply started typing as God was speaking. I am Cynthia Bolton, a happily married mother of two beautiful children and a wife of a God sent man, only a vessel being used by God.

Thanks to the Readers, I hope you were inspired.

CYNTHIA MARIE BOLTON